HEIDI GOENNEL
I Pretend

TAMBOURINE BOOKS   NEW YORK

FOR PETER

Library of Congress Cataloging in Publication Data
Goennel, Heidi. I pretend / Heidi Goennel. — 1st ed   p. cm.
Summary: Using her imagination, a child can have a tea party
with a mouse, be a mermaid or a witch, walk in outer space,
or ride on a flying carpet. [1. Imagination—Fiction.] I. Title.
PZ7.G554Iaac 1995 [E]—dc20 94-28129 CIP AC
ISBN 0-688-13592-7. — ISBN 0-688-13593-5 (lib.)
1 3 5 7 9 10 8 6 4 2
First edition

Sometimes I pretend that I'm having a tea party

with the mouse who lives behind the wall.

While I play in the sand by the ocean,

I pretend I am a beautiful mermaid.

While I help mix and mix a can of green paint,

I pretend I'm stirring a witch's brew.

When I walk on my hands and try cartwheels,

I pretend that I'm walking in outer space.

Sometimes when I play with Pepe,

I pretend she's a fierce and bold tiger!

When the ghost stories at camp get too scary,

I pretend that I'm on a deserted island.

I like to pretend that my new toboggan

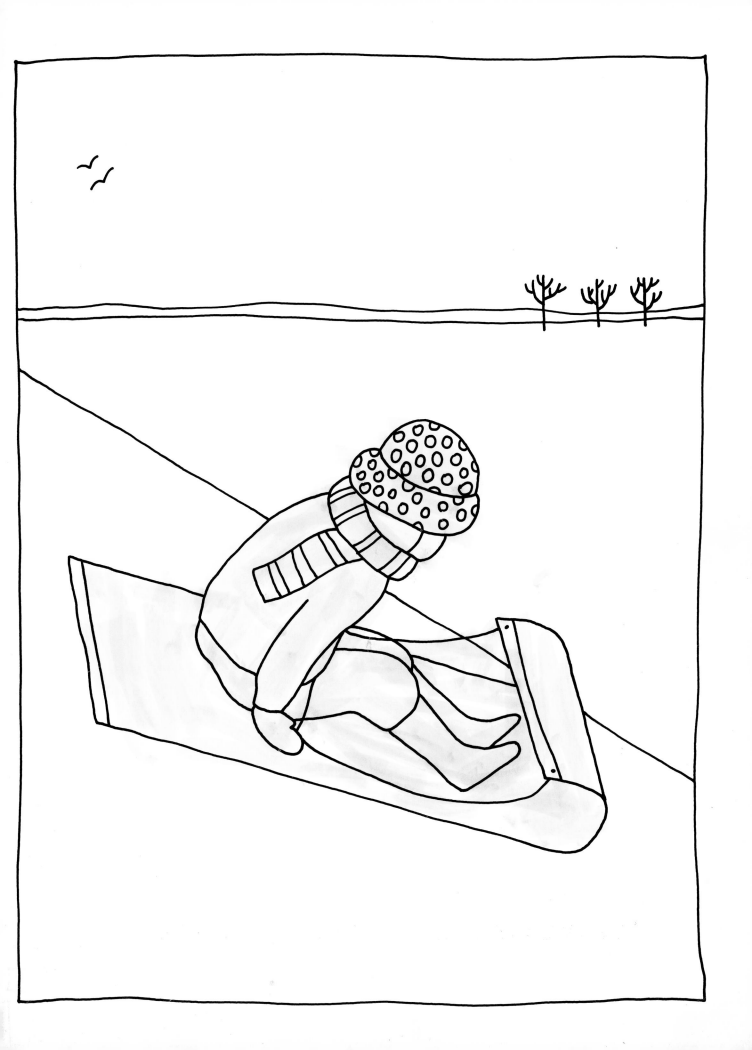

is really a flying carpet . . . and off we go!